LITTLE
CHRIS

originated by Roger Hargreaves

Written and illustrated by Adam Hargreaves

MR. MEN   LITTLE MISS

PRICE STERN SLOAN
An Imprint of Penguin Group (USA) Inc.

Little Miss Christmas™ and copyright © 2005 by THOIP (a Chorion company). All rights reserved worldwide. First published in the United States in 2008 by Price Stern Sloan, a division of Penguin Young Readers Group, 345 Hudson Street, New York, New York 10014. *PSS!* is a registered trademark of Penguin Group (USA) Inc. Manufactured in China.

ISBN 978-0-8431-2669-3   10 9 8 7 6 5 4 3

Little Miss Christmas lives in an igloo at the North Pole, next door to her uncle, Santa Claus, and a long, long way from her brother, Mr. Christmas.

Little Miss Christmas works for Santa Claus. Her job is wrapping all the presents before Santa delivers them on Christmas Eve.

As you might imagine, there are an awful lot of presents to wrap—it takes her all year long. And as much as Little Miss Christmas loves her job, there are times when wrapping presents day in and day out can get a bit boring.

Last year, after nearly a whole year buried in wrapping paper and sticky tape, Little Miss Christmas decided that she deserved a vacation.

She had nearly finished wrapping all the presents and thought that it would not do any harm for Santa to wrap the last few himself.

To make it easier for him, she called her brother at the South Pole and asked him to come and help.

Mr. Christmas flew up to the North Pole in his magic flying teapot on the day Little Miss Christmas left for her vacation.

"I won't be back until the day before Christmas Eve, so you have to make sure you finish wrapping the last of the presents," Little Miss Christmas reminded them just before she boarded her plane.

"Don't worry," boomed Santa Claus. "We've got plenty of time! We'll have them all wrapped long before you return."

The next morning, after a breakfast of Christmas pudding on toast, Santa led Mr. Christmas into the wrapping room and they set to work.

"This isn't going to take any time at all," said Santa an hour later. "In fact, we've got plenty of time left. How about a game of golf?"

"Good idea," said Mr. Christmas.

And so the two of them played golf for the rest of the day.

The following morning, they settled down to work. But after an hour, Santa Claus piped up again, "How about going reindeer racing? We've got plenty of time left to do this."

"Good idea," agreed Mr. Christmas.

And the two of them spent the rest of the day racing reindeer across the ice.

The next day, they did not even reach the wrapping room.

"We've still got plenty of time to finish that wrapping. Shall we go fishing today?" suggested Santa at breakfast.

"Good idea," said Mr. Christmas eagerly.

And so it continued.

While Little Miss Christmas lay on a beach in the Christmas Islands (where else?!), blissfully unaware of what was going on, Santa Claus and Mr. Christmas were spending a lot of time having fun and very little time wrapping presents.

So you will not be surprised to learn that the wrapping had not been finished by the time Little Miss Christmas returned from her vacation.

"What have you two been doing all this time?" exclaimed Little Miss Christmas when she saw the huge pile of unwrapped presents.

Santa Claus and Mr. Christmas sheepishly studied their feet, unable to look Little Miss Christmas in the eye.

"How are we ever going to get all this done by tomorrow evening?" she continued angrily.

It was then that she suddenly had an idea.

A brilliant idea.

"We can ask all the Mr. Men and Little Misses to help us! And you can go and pick them up in your teapot!" she cried, pointing at Mr. Christmas.

By teatime, Mr. Christmas had collected as many of the Mr. Men and Little Misses as he could find and brought them to the North Pole.

They all worked right through the night, although Little Miss Christmas had to be careful about which jobs she gave them.

Mr. Bump was only allowed to wrap teddy bears because he kept breaking the other presents he was given.

And Little Miss Bossy had to keep a careful eye on Little Miss Naughty to stop her from wrapping nasty surprises in her presents.

Not everything went quite as planned.

Mr. Muddle kept writing "Happy Easter" on the labels.

And Little Miss Helpful tried very hard to be helpful, but got into a lot of trouble with the sticky tape.

Mr. Forgetful kept forgetting to put presents in his boxes.

And there was no mistaking the presents wrapped by Mr. Messy!

However, by lunchtime on Christmas Eve, all the presents were wrapped and labeled and packed away in Santa Claus's sleigh.

"Thank you so much," said Little Miss Christmas to everyone. "I don't know what we would have done without your help. There would have been a lot of empty spaces under a lot of Christmas trees. Now we just need Santa Claus! Has anyone seen him?"

But nobody had.

Eventually, Little Miss Christmas found him playing cards—with Mr. Christmas, of course!

"Quick, quick!" she cried. "You're going to be late!"

"Don't worry, don't worry," chuckled Santa.

"We've got plenty of time!"